9

For my daughter
Xandria B.C

For all the little ones
at Clifton Tots P.B

First published in 2016
by Scholastic Children's Books
Euston House, 24 Eversholt Street,
London NW1 1DB
a division of Scholastic Ltd
www.scholastic.co.uk
London ~ New York ~ Toronto ~ Sydney ~ Auckland
Mexico City ~ New Delhi ~ Hong Kong

Text copyright © 2016 Bernadette Carelse
Illustrations copyright © 2016 Paula Bowles

PB ISBN 978 1407 16718 3

10 9 8 7 6 5 4 3 2 1

My Mindful Little One
~Bedtime~

Written by Dr Bernadette Carelse

Illustrated by Paula Bowles

Introduction:

What is mindfulness?

Mindfulness is a way of engaging the attention and bringing awareness into whatever is happening in the present moment. It can also be a way of simply letting go of whatever may be distracting you and focusing the attention with gentleness and kindness.

Mindfulness is an awareness that arises from opening up to, and turning towards, moment-by-moment experiences in an open-hearted, kindly, non-judgmental way [1]. It is developed through formal practices done sitting, moving or lying down, and informal ones that can be integrated into everyday life.

What are the benefits for me and my child?

Mindfulness can bring many benefits, but essentially a sense of being connected to lived experiences, moment by moment. Research shows that it can lead to increased and improved attachment between parents and their children. Attachment is key in children developing their own sense of identity and self-confidence.

Mindfulness is also a form of mental training that works for both children and adults. There is good evidence from neuroscience and brain-imaging studies with adults that regularly practising mindfulness meditation can help reduce stress, lift mood and be a source of support through challenges that families regularly face.

Mindfulness also benefits children from all age ranges, regardless of whether or not they have any mental or physical health problems.

Studies have found that:
- Mindfulness is well-received and found to be enjoyable [2].
- Mindfulness can improve mental, emotional and physical health and well-being [3].
- Mindfulness can lead to better thinking and attention skills [4,5].
- Mindfulness can help reduce stress [6] and difficult feelings, such as anxiety and low mood [7]. This can lead to improved sleep, a greater sense of calmness and confidence, self-awareness and empathy.

How do I use this book with my child?

There are many ways to use this book and the key is to discover what works for you and your child. These suggestions are offered as guides for you to try out as you wish:

Take care of your needs too.

It may help to begin by pausing, and taking time to notice whatever is happening in your own body. Check if you have any needs of your own that need fulfilling first. Sometimes, we get so busy that we forget to look after ourselves. The first step is to tune in to how we are feeling and to do what needs to be done in this moment.

The day has come and gone so fast,
So many things now in the past.
And now is now. It's time for bed.
Time to rest and lay down my head.

Today I did many
things that were fun.

I played inside and
out in the sun.

I played some games,
you played with me.

Now let's pause,
breathe and just be.

Before my bed, I have my bath.
I love to wash, to splash, to laugh.
I wash my feet. I wash my toes.
I wash my face. I wash my nose.

The water's not too cold or hot.
I wash and wash, now time to stop.

I feel the towel wrapped all around,
I feel my toes touching the ground.

I feel my breathing, just like the sea

In comes a wave, as high as can be.

Then gently and slowly

down it goes.

Out flows the breath, out through my nose.

Upon each breath imagine a boat.
Rock it gently to keep it afloat.

Steadily floating up, floating down,
Travelling onwards to its home town.

While I'm breathing I look all around –
By freshly looking new things are found.
Beyond this book, I look and I see
All sorts of things that are here with me.

Here is the room, the walls and the door,
Maybe there are some toys on the floor.
Cuddling up and reading with me,
Gently we look – each other we see.

I remember them all, one by one –
Those in my life, with whom I have fun.

Some are family, others are not.
I love some a little – some a lot.

I remember each day that comes and goes.
All the dreams I will dream, nobody knows.
Each moment is precious, each single now,
All coming and going, who only knows how?

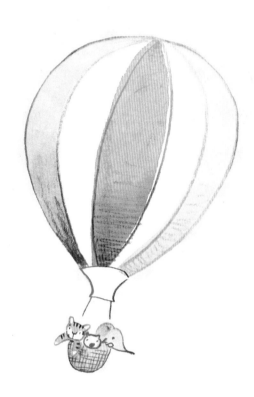